Gingerbread
man /
Baking.

HRA
Storytime

not For Loan.

First published 1999 by Walker Books Ltd
87 Vauxhall Walk, London SE11 5HJ

2 4 6 8 10 9 7 5 3 1

© 1999 Lucy Cousins

Based on the Audio Visual series "Maisy". A King Rollo Films Production for
PolyGram Visual Programming. Original script by Andrew Brenner.

This book has been typeset in Lucy Cousins typeface.

Printed in Hong Kong

British Library Cataloguing in Publication Data
A catalogue record for this book is
available from the British Library.

0-7445-6767-X (hb)
0-7445-7218-5 (pb)

Maisy Makes Gingerbread

Lucy Cousins

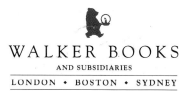

WALKER BOOKS

AND SUBSIDIARIES

LONDON • BOSTON • SYDNEY

Maisy is in her kitchen today.

She is going to make gingerbread.

Maisy needs flour, sugar, butter, eggs and ginger.

Maisy mixes everything together.

She rolls out the mixture and cuts different shapes.

Maisy puts the gingerbread into the oven.

Maisy licks the bowl while the gingerbread is cooking.

Then she washes up.
Ding-dong!
That's the doorbell!
Who can it be?

It's Charley and Tallulah!

Just in time for afternoon tea.

Yum, yum!
Nice gingerbread,
Maisy.

If you're crazy for Maisy, you'll love these other books featuring Maisy and her friends.

Other titles
Maisy's ABC • Maisy Goes to Bed • Maisy Goes to the Playground
Maisy Goes Swimming • Maisy Goes to Playschool
Maisy's House • Happy Birthday, Maisy • Maisy at the Farm